For Gaby and Dory who will soon be
All Asleep

First published in 2007
by Hodder Children's Books

Text and illustrations copyright © Joanna Walsh 2007

Hodder Children's Books
338 Euston Road, London NW1 3BH

Hodder Children's Books Australia
Hachette Children's Books
Level 17/207 Kent Street, Sydney, NSW 2000

A catalogue record of this book is available from the British Library.

ISBN: 9780340911334
10 9 8 7 6 5 4 3 2 1

Printed in China

Hodder Children's Books is a division of Hachette Children's Books.

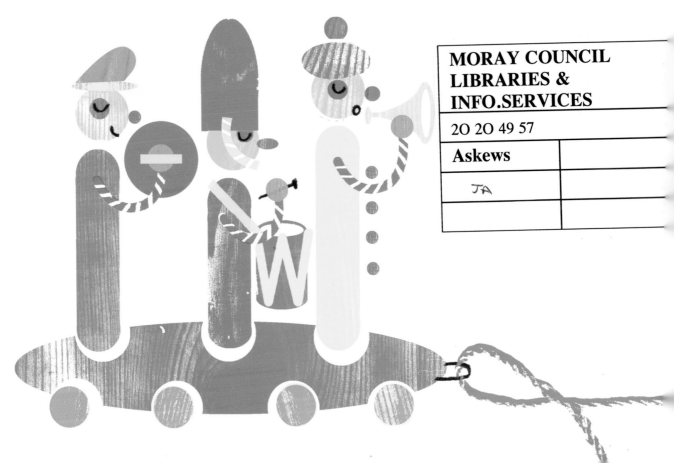

All Asleep

Joanna Walsh

Say nothing,
take a peep,
the babies are
all fast asleep.

All babies? Small babies?

Tall babies?
Yes and...

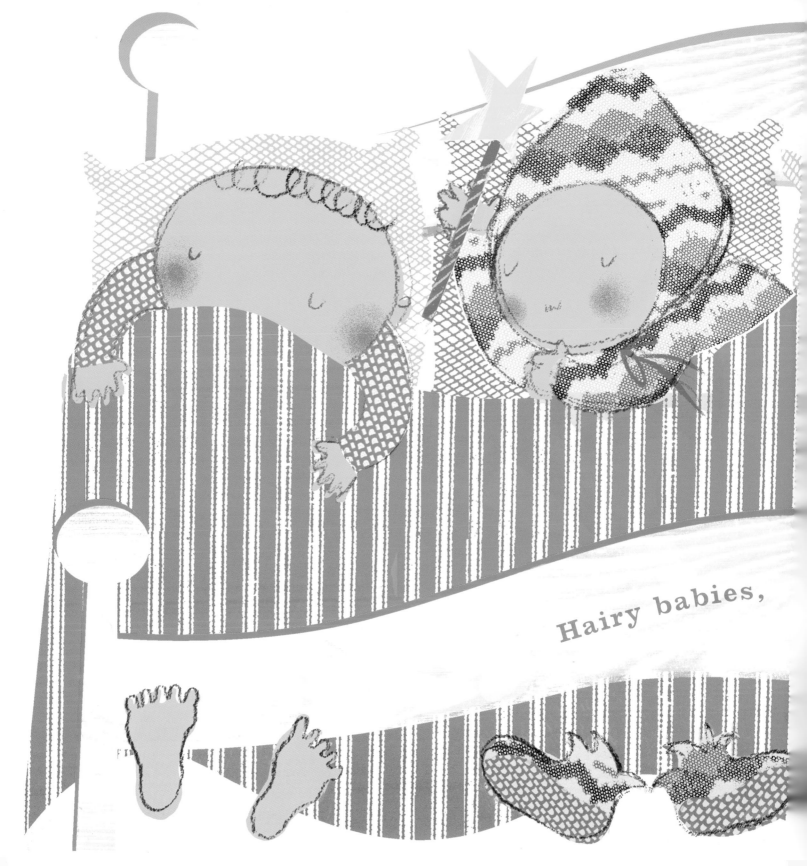

Hairy babies,

fairy babies, beary babies.

Babies on mummies
and on daddies' tummies.
Babies on grannies, sisters,
brothers and others.

In Babygros, with bows
and stripy toes.

Babies who sleep in
cribs, in bibs.

Babies in cradles
able to rock.

Babies at kitchen tables.
Babies in one sock.

Babies in tiny flats with cats,

sleeping in
high-rise towers
for hours
and hours...

Babies on
mountain tops
in shops,
sleeping with
oxes and in
cardboard boxes.

Babies in aeroplanes

and speeding trains.

Babies in ships upon
the deep blue sea.

Fingers to lips,
'Shhhh, babies fast asleep.'

Babies in cars.
One baby in a
balloon under
the stars

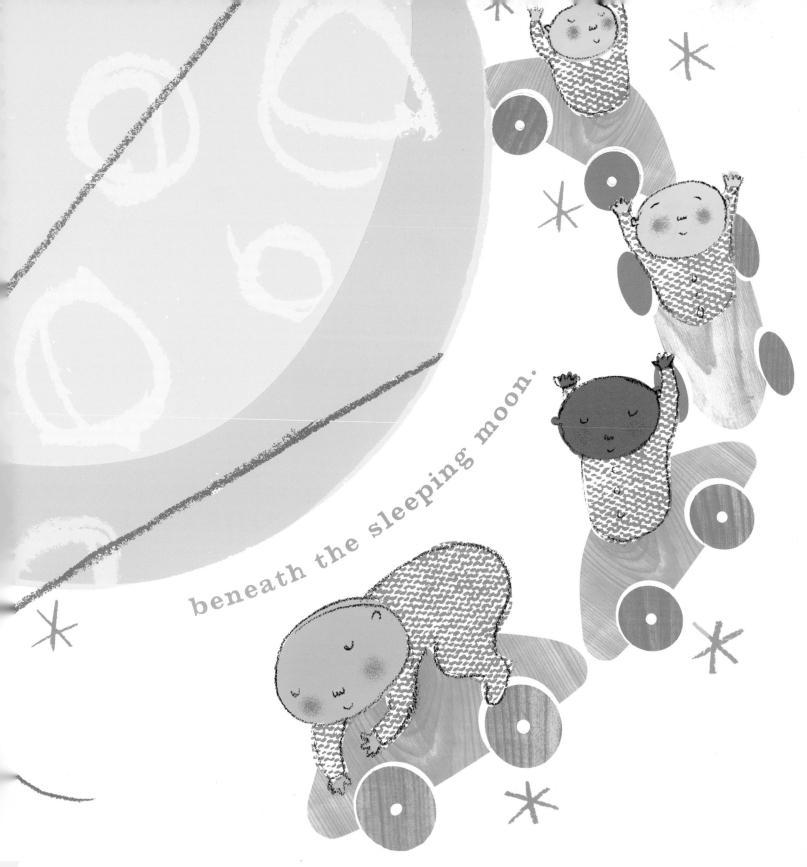

beneath the sleeping moon.

Even the babies
who wake up all night
are sleeping now,
are sleeping tight.

Say nothing, quietly creep,
the babies are all fast asleep.